Am I Black on the Inside?

Alaina McMurtry

TABLE OF CONTENTS

CHAPTER ONE

Meet Aiden

Hi. My name is Aiden. I'm 10 years old and in the fifth grade. I have three brothers, two older and one baby brother. We all live in our house with mom and dad.

We live in a white house on a cul-de-sac. A cul-de-sac is a dead-end street where cars can't go through. It's fun to play outside in the street, because we don't have to worry about cars driving through. I like to ride my bike, race, play football and catch sometimes with my brothers and my neighbors.

Two of my neighbors have swimming pools. They invite us over sometimes to swim with them. I love to swim! I passed the swim test at our gym pool to get my wristband last summer. Some people swim when it's cold outside! We can only swim if it's 80 degrees or warmer. I wish we had a pool. I would swim all the time!

I walk to my school when my daddy doesn't take me sometimes, when it's warm outside. My school is about three blocks away from our house. I have lots of friends at my school. Having friends is important to me. I worry that people won't like me though. Sometimes some of them talk bad to me. I don't say anything most of the time, because I want them to like me. I want to be one of the cool kids!

My school is a mix of all kinds of people; black, white, brown, all different kinds. The teachers are mostly white though, except the music teacher. She's a good teacher but a little mean.

Most of my friends are in another class but I get to see them at recess and we play football together. That's my very favorite sport. I play on a tackle football team too! I played quarterback last year. This year, I'm playing both defense and offense. I play football in the spring league and in the fall. I love it that much!

I used to play baseball. I was one of the fastest pitchers last season. My aim wasn't the best though. I hit someone in the head. The ball bounced off his helmet, all the way over the tall fence behind him! He wasn't hurt at all though. Whew! He just took his base. "Ooops!" I smiled a little. My coach said "Aiden. it's not funny!" It was a tiiiny bit funny though.

In school, I spend most of my time in Ms. Lawler's class but we go to another class for math and reading. This is supposed to get us ready to change classes in middle school next year. It's okay I guess. I just wish my friends were in my class, and my teacher wasn't so mean.

CHAPTER TWO

Glasses

I'm having kind of a bad day today. There are these boys in my class that say mean things about me. One called me ugly because I wear glasses and the others laughed. It embarrassed me and made me sad. When I was sad, I started to think that they were right maybe I am ugly. I don't like my glasses.

Then I remembered what my mom says when I start feeling sad and thinking about bad stuff: "Aiden, when you find your self starting to think negative things, you **immediately** have to chase those bad thoughts away by thinking good thoughts!" Light chases away darkness she tells me.

"Good thoughts like what?" I asked her.

"Well, what makes you smile?" She asked me once. Hmmm, I thought, "Football makes me smile mommy" I said. She told me to think about how it would feel throwing the winning touchdown or breaking a tackle to score at the buzzer!

So that's what I did! You know what? It made me feel better! When I was thinking good thoughts, the bad thoughts just disappeared! Just like when I turn on a light in a dark room, light *does* chase away the darkness!

Sometimes it's hard to force myself to think good thoughts but it's important that I do. Thinking about things that make me smile makes me feel better and the way I feel IS important.

CHAPTER THREE

Choose!

In fifth grade, I get to walk home from school by myself! So, after school one day, I say goodbye to my friends and start to walk home.

On the way, some of the cool guys ask me to play football with them. *YES*!!! I was really excited because I love football and I really wanted these friends to like me!

Then I remembered that I am supposed to go straight home from school every day and do my homework and chores. I did have some math homework but mom and dad were still at work so would they *even know* if I stayed to play? My older brother Logan is home but I bet he's taking a nap. Plus, mom and dad want me to make friends anyway, right? I thought to myself, of course they do!

I really wanted to, so I went and played football with the cool boys! You know what? I played great! I threw two touchdowns *and even* got a pick six on defense!!!! Nobody could catch me! They started calling me "Bolt," like the fastest man in the world. I LOVED it! I felt great playing with them! The cool boys liked **me**!

When we finished playing, I straightened my glasses, wiped some of the dirt off my clothes and walked home with a smile plastered all over my face. As I got closer to my house though, I noticed the garage door was open and both my mom and dad's cars were inside!!!!! I had an instant sick feeling in my stomach. Oh no! I thought! Crying and praying, I said "God please help me to not get in trouble!!! Please please please please!"

I tried to walk in the door like nothing was wrong. "Hi Mommy, hi Dad" I said. But my mom and dad were standing right there asking where I had been? "You were supposed to be home by 3:30, where have you been!?!" mommy said. They looked soooo mad! It was 4:15.

"Ummm, mommy, daddy, don't be mad, I was walking home after school and my new friends asked me to play a game of football with them. They were the *COOL GUYS* mommy, and they wanted **me** to play with them! I know how much you want me to make friends right? So I played with them." I whined. "I'm sorry."

She looked at my dad and he said, "you know what the rules are don't you?" "Yes Sir" I said. "Then why did you choose to ignore them?" "I don't know." "Ok, well go to your room and I'll come deal with you later" said my dad. Oh my God! I know what that means. I hurried up and went to my room. I put on four more pairs of underwear and a pair of shorts under my jeans real quick.

I was right! I got a spanking and couldn't go outside and play for a whole week!!!! But the cool boys liked **me**!!!! I smiled anyway.

CHAPTER FOUR

Purpose

Since I couldn't go outside or play my video games, mom thought it would be a good idea to have me think about what my purpose is.......... "What?"

She said I should figure out what my purpose is for fifth grade. Then she said, also, think about what your purpose is for playing football. "Ugggh!" I said that *after* she left of course. She didn't hear me (I'm not crazy)!

I don't even know what **purpose** means! So I got my phone out and went to one of my dictionary apps and this is what I found:

Purpose: ~noun

1. the reason something exists or is done, made, used, etc.

2. the intended or desired result; end; goal

So.... What is my intended or desired result; end; goal for fifth grade?

I thought about it for a moment. I don't think it's to make friends, or to have fun. I guess I want to pass fifth grade so I can get to sixth grade! That's my purpose!

I know my mom though, and it can't be that easy. Ummm, well I would like to get good grades too I guess.

"Ok mom", I yelled to her down the hall, "My purpose for the fifth grade is to get good grades and get to the sixth grade!!!" "Good!" she yelled back, "Now what are the steps you need to take to achieve that purpose?" "Moooom!" I whined, putting my head down on my desk! "What do you mean?"

Mom comes into my room folding baby Ethan's clothes and sits down on my bed. "Son, we have to be clear on what our purpose is for everything we do. Using your mind to think is the one thing **only YOU** are in complete control of. Once you are clear on your purpose you will know what to do when you get to a crossroads; like you did when you decided to play football after school today. Once you are clear on your purpose, you will ask yourself, which of these decisions will serve your purpose?"

"Do you understand?" She asked. "Not really." I said.

"Okay, you say you want to make good grades in school and graduate to the sixth grade right?" "Right" I say. "Ok, if your purpose is to make good grades, what decision would best support your purpose; going to play football or coming straight home doing your homework?"

"Hommmmeworrrk "I say rolling my eyes. But I'm starting to understand.

"But mom, I have a purpose for football too!" "I'm sure you do son, but you have to prioritize. In order to play football, you still have to have what?" She asks. "Good grades" I mumble. "Exactly!" "You think for yourself. You choose your own path," my mom told me. "But there are consequences for every decision; good or bad."

She asked me to figure out my purpose for school, for my relationship with my family; at home and for my chores. So I got to work. It was kind of fun actually! It wasn't like I could go out and play anyway... I was grounded!

Once my loooong, boring week of punishment was over, my new friends (the cool guys) asked me to play football with them again after school! I thought about that crossroads mom talked about.

I think for myself; I choose my own path

What is my purpose? My purpose is to get good grades so I can go to sixth grade! So I told them I had to go home do my homework and chores and then I would come back and play football with them. It feels good to make a decision that *supports* my purpose.

CHAPTER FIVE

Colton

The boys that make fun of me at school are bullies. They are mean to everybody. When they laugh at me because I get an answer wrong in class, I get embarrassed. It makes me not want to answer questions in class any more. So now when my teacher calls on me, I don't say anything. That's a decision I made.

So it turns out that every decision I make is a "crossroads" decision. We make decisions all day, every day. We make them super fast. Every time we decide to say something or do something, we are moving either one step closer to our purpose or one step away from it.

One day at recess one of those mean boys pushed me and called me dumb. He laughed and other people joined in and laughed too. Even some of the people I thought were my friends!

I tried to think good thoughts immediately. Think good thoughts, think good thoughts! I tried really hard but I was so embarrassed.

None of the teachers saw them do it and I didn't want to tell on them because that would just make them bother me even more. So I didn't say anything. I didn't do anything. The crossroads choice I made was to stay quiet.

Since I didn't do anything or tell anyone, they kept being mean to me. They would call me names and push me.

One day Colton hit me. Colton is white. I know by now that if I hit him back, I'm going to be the one that gets in trouble. So I don't hit him back.

I have two older brothers. I know *how* to fight. I just don't like to fight and I didn't want to get in trouble.

I went home feeling really sad. My oldest brother Dillon saw me and asked me what was wrong. "Nothing" I said, close to tears. "Somebody messing with you at school?" My brother Logan asked me. "You need me to talk to them?" He asked making a fist? "No Logan." I said and turned to leave.

Dillon who is in college was home for something that day and he told me to come sit next to him on the couch.

"Hey little bro, you okay?" He put his arm around me. "Kinda" I whispered. "Colton has been pushing me at school, and today he hit me" I told Dillon. He looked surprised but then he said, "Well you know how we are suppose to deal with that right?" I look at him, "No, how?"

He starts to tell me how: Both me and Logan dealt with this same thing at that school. Our parents told us to do this:

1.   If someone hits you, tell him to stop and tell the teacher.

   I interrupt him telling him "I don't want to be a snitch." He says, "I know, I felt the exact same way! But you will understand **WHY** you have to tell the teacher in a minute."

2.   If they hit you a second time, tell them to stop **AND** tell them if they hit you again, you are going to hit them back! Then, as much as you don't want to, you have to tell the teacher again. This time you have to also tell the teacher that if they hit you a third time you *will* hit them back!

   Why do I have to keep snitching? Ugggh!!! "You'll see," he said.

3.   If they are dumb enough to hit you a third time Aiden, BEAT THEM UP!!!! Don't just hit them back. You have to beat them up!

Just as he told me the last part my mom walked in. Apparently she had heard the whole thing too. She said: "if you don't whoop them, I'm going to whoop YOU" and walked on through the room!

Dillon laughed and said "Yep! At that point, you have to fight back or you will be bullied forever."

"That's why you have to make sure you tell the teacher when it happens son." Mommy came back, grabbing my hand. "You have to give your teacher the opportunity to put an end to it before it gets to the point of you fighting back. If you don't, **YOU** will be the one to get in trouble for fighting when you hit them back." "You know how it works, black boys can't do the same things as other boys. It's seen as aggressive, even when you're fighting back".

Then she said, "It's just as important to tell the teacher that if they hit you again, you will hit them back" "Why?" I asked. Mommy actually said, that if I tell them my intentions, then the problem is no longer between the boy and me it's then between my parents and the school.

She said she and dad would take it from there.

CHAPTER SIX

Pipeline

I got my math test grade back today. I got a 'D' on it. Stupid Colton got a 'B' and he was all in my face about it at recess. "Leave me alone Colton, I am not in the mood!" I told him. The test was on angles and stuff. I'm terrible at math and I hate it! My Nana makes me go to tutoring so I can get better. I hate that more than I hate school!!

I got in trouble at home for getting the stupid 'D', and I didn't even care. I hate math and I will never be good at it!

While grounded, guess what? Mom told me to think about, my stupid purpose again!!! "Did getting that 'D' support your purpose for school Aiden; or move you away from it?" I didn't say anything but I know the answer. I'm mad! "Son...?" she asked. "It didn't support my purpose mommy and I don't care! Math is hard and I hate it!"

"I see", mom said and she left the room. (I thought she was going to get the belt. She's good for that!)

"While she walked away, I heard her say, "Watch what comes out of your mouth little boy. Your words are powerful!"

She comes back and hands me an article called "The Grade School to Prison Pipeline". I didn't feel like reading it but I knew if I didn't she would get all mad.

It said something about boys that look like me and how the decision for our paths are made right around my age.

The "system" decides if I will need a college dorm room or a prison cell when I grow up. They decide that at around age 9 years old it said!!!! Some of the things they look at are grades and whether or not we get in trouble in school. Then as we grow up, our paths are pretty much *guided in that direction*. PRISON?!?!?!

But, I thought I was in charge of my path? I thought it was my choice?

I wonder if white boys have a pipeline.

I go downstairs to the kitchen and ask mom and dad some questions. "What does this mean daddy? Am I going to prison?" "No way!!!" my dad says. "The only person that can determine your future is you Aiden! The reason mom showed you that article is so you can see that getting good grades IS important in how society sees you."

"The system is not on our side son and we have to do twice as much as other people to get half the opportunities."

"I'm just a kid though, how can **I** be a candidate for prison at 10?" "Sonshine, (that's what mom calls all of us because we are her "sons and I guess we shine...") you and only you can determine how far you go in this life. Your brain is the only thing you and you alone have complete control over, but it's extremely important that you understand how the world sees you."

"Do you know why I named you and your brothers Dillon, Logan, Aiden and Ethan?" Mom asked me.

"Because they all end in 'N'?" I asked. She laughed, "No son, we gave you those names first because they all have very powerful meanings and secondly because we didn't want people to be able to look at your written name and know you're black."

"This is the choice we made. It's not the only choice, but it was our choice. There are many different considerations concerning naming our children.

Naming ceremonies have historically been an important rite of passage in our community. Some people choose powerful ethnic names that have beautiful meanings that reflect the rich, powerful and resilient heritage that I am extremely proud of. We are a very special and blessed people! Choosing a name is a personal preference. There is not a *wrong* choice."

Mom went on, "Considering where we live and how we are viewed, dad and I made a different choice."

"We thought about your resumes, your applications to college, for apartments, mortgages and credit cards. Those things are not important to you now, but they will be very important to you later. We did our part, the rest is up to you!"

"I don't want to go to prison mommy I whined...I'm NOT going to prison mommy!" "I know you're not son. I just need you to understand how important getting good grades is, even now."

"I'm going back to my room to study." I yelled.

I studied so hard. I came home from school each day and studied some more. I studied for math, science, history and language arts.

There were still some things that I didn't understand so I asked for help. I went to tutoring without complaining because now I understood that our parents are just trying to make sure we make good decisions in life. Now I understand that the world sees me as a bad boy before I even open my mouth just because my skin is brown. I have to be careful in everything I do. Do all black boys and girls have to understand this? I wonder.

CHAPTER SEVEN

Reality

The next test I took in math was not as hard as the other one but a couple questions got a little confusing. I thought I understood it but I only got a 'B' on it! It was better than the 'D' but I thought I was going to get an 'A'.

I remembered my purpose and studied so hard. I refused to give up! I make my own decisions. I am the only one that has control of my thinking. I get to choose my own path! I choose to get good grades!

On my way to lunch with my class, my teacher pulled me aside and asked me if I cheated on the test. He (my math teacher is a man) said I was more like a 'D' student and he was surprised that I got a 'B' on the last test. "WHAT!?!?" "No sir. I didn't cheat! I just studied and tried really hard" He said he believed me but......I'm not sure. I thought he would be proud of me for trying hard.

At the dinner table later, I told my family I got a 'B' on my test and they were really happy for me. Even Logan, who is so mean to me, said "good job, Bro!" Then I told them what my teacher asked me about cheating and everybody stopped talking. They just looked at each other and got really quiet. I could tell they were mad.

Dad took me to school the next day and went in instead of dropping me off like he usually did. He met with my teacher and the principal. I'm not sure what happened at that meeting but the teacher apologized to me later and never asked me that again.

I'm starting to see that I really do have to work twice as hard to get half as much! I'm going to study every night until I get an 'A' on all my tests! I'll show that teacher!

CHAPTER EIGHT

Enough!

I was doing much better in math! It wasn't so hard once I started studying. My other grades were always OK but now even those were As and Bs! Walking to school one day though, I got really sad. I wondered why God made me black. Why did he make white people better than us? Everything "black" is bad and everything "white" is good. Think about that.

Are we black on the inside I wondered? Is there something wrong with us? Why do we have to work so hard just to prove to people that we are good? My pastor said we were made in God's image. What does He look like?

About that time, Colton and Billy walk up to me. "Did you have a good weekend Aiden? Billy said laughing. "Leave me alone" I told them. We were at school now passing the playground where a few students were playing before school. "Or what?" Colton asked, "You're going to beat me up?" They both cracked up laughing!

(Remember he had already hit me twice and I told him if he did it again, I would have to beat him up.)

"Yes" I said and kept walking. Colton handed Billy his backpack and came and stood in front of me. I walked around him trying to get inside the school. He put his foot out, pushed me and tripped me! It wasn't a "hit" exactly but I was so tired of them messing with me!!!!

I got up and balled up my fists and punched him in the stomach over and over and over until someone pulled me off of him. My glasses fell off when he tripped me so I couldn't really see who pulled me off of him. Colton started crying like a little baby and everybody saw it.

Then the Principal came and took me, Colton and Billy to the office. Someone brought my glasses and left them at the desk.

They started asking **me** all kinds of questions and telling me how I am going to be in big trouble because **I** hurt **him**! He told me to apologize to Colton right now! "NO!!!" I said. I'm not going to apologize to him. They bother me every single day and no one has ever told them to stop, or to apologize to me!

"I'm calling your parents!!!! You better believe you are going to get suspended for this", he smirked!! "I don't know why kids **like you** are so violent! Always fighting! We have a zero-tolerance policy for fighting at this school," he says.

"Good, call my parents because I am NOT apologizing to him."

They got there so fast! They came all the way from work too! I can tell they are furious but they are acting like they are very calm.

The Principal said to my parents, "I asked Aiden why he hit Colton and he said 'he deserved it'!!!! I don't know what kind of school you think this is Mr. and Mrs........."

"Let me stop you right there" my mother said as calmly as she could. She brought her shaky finger up in the Principal's face! Uh oh! I thought! My dad grabbed her gently and took control of the situation. She had tears in her eyes now.

"Call Aiden's teacher to the office" Dad said. Mom was hugging me now and I was crying too!

My teacher came to the office and the grown-ups started talking. The teacher admitted that I had told him Colton and Billy were bullying me for weeks! He also admitted that I told him that if it happened again, I was going to beat him up.

"I had too! I said, If I didn't, **I** was going to get in trouble at home! My mommy said if I didn't......." Mom gave me a look that said, BE QUIET!!!! I stopped talking!

"Colton," the principal bent down and said gently like he would break, "Did you hit Aiden before? Tell me the truth buddy," he said so sweetly. "Yes" Colton said looking down and still half crying. Billy, did you? "Yes" Billy admitted too.

The Principal straightened up and looked at my parents and said, "Well......he's not suspended but the manner in which Aiden hit Colton was excessive and unacceptable. He hit him many times in the stomach, witnesses said. I'm going to ask you to take him home for the rest of the day, as the boys are all very upset."

Mom and dad asked to speak to the Principal and the teacher alone. When they came out, my mom had been crying and the teacher looked terrified. I can only imagine what happened.

As mom, dad and I walked to the car, mom said "You are not in trouble Aiden because you told the teacher all along what was going on." "You gave the grown-ups a chance to rectify the situation and they didn't. You are not in trouble at school or at home" mom told me when we got to the car.

"I'm very proud of you son" my daddy said. "I know you don't like to fight. It's always a last resort but if you follow the steps we've set out for you, you shouldn't have to fight at all. After today, you might not ever have to fight again," dad said half smiling. "Did all the other kids see you beat Colton's……." mom shot dad a look with her eyebrows up. Dad just smiled.

I hope you understand why it's important to tell the teacher now" Mom interrupted. "I understand," I said.

Then we went for ice cream.

CHAPTER NINE

In My Image

"Why did God make white people better than us? I asked my parents.

"God made everyone equal son. It's not God that treats us differently son, **people** that do that. Somewhere along the way, because of how black people got to this land, it was decided that we were less valuable than other people. We are not! We are beautiful, loving, kind and creative. We are strong and resilient, powerful and great. The truth is, it's up to you," they told me. "You get to choose!"

"God made you in His image Aiden. He made you just like Him. He gave YOU the ability to do some of the same things Jesus did." It even say so in the Bible."

"He gave you the ability to create your own future, think for yourself, have what you want to have, and be who you want to be!" Mom explained.

"You can succeed even if there are barriers in your way. NEVER GIVE UP" my parents told me. "In this world, because of the color of your skin, you will have to work twice as hard to get half of what others get; and no one will care that it's unfair. That has never stopped our people before and it won't stop us now. You were given the power to create your own future, determine your own outcomes. Believe it! Start right now!"

"How do I start?" I asked.

Remember when I told you what to do when you find yourself thinking bad thoughts? "Yes ma'am, I'm supposed to think of something that makes me happy."

"Exactly! You should do this the exact moment you realize your thoughts have gone to a negative place and you feel bad. The way you **feel** is important. It's important because like attracts like." "Huh"? I said to my mom.

"Things attract things that are like them. Positive thoughts and feelings attract positive thoughts and feelings. Negative thoughts and feelings; attract more negative thoughts and feelings. If we dwell on things long enough, they start to manifest into real things either positive or negative. So always stay positive. Do what you can to make yourself **feel** happy!"

"Okay, I think I get it. I'm going to see how many good thoughts I can think today." "Awesome! Don't forget your purpose Aiden. You get to choose it all!"

"What is one thing that you want right now"? "I want to be the starting wide-receiver for my football team."

"Okay, do you think that might be considered a purpose that you have?" "Yes!" "I think so too," mom said to me.

"Take some quiet time every day and think how it might be to be the starting Receiver. How would that look? What would you do? What would you wear? How hard do you have to practice? How much fun would it be? How would you act? Then finally, how would it *feel*? Think about it would make you feel often!"

"That's how you do it for *anything* you want!"

"Mommy, I want to go to Ohio State for football too." "Well you know how to make it happen now Sonshine. Oh! You have to have good grades to get into Ohio State you know? Now, go make it happen! Work toward it everyday. Consider it at every crossroad." She said.

I understand now why it is so important that I keep trying. It's important that I never give up. I am going to keep studying and make A's in all my classes. I'm going to keep my purpose in my mind and never ever give up! Even if I fail, I will keep trying. Every single time!

I go to my room and lay on my bed. Even though there are some people that will still think I'm bad, it's up to me! God made me in His image! Now I know what he looks like! God made me to be just like ME!!!

Made in His Image

Made in the USA
San Bernardino, CA
10 May 2019